This

MOUSE ❈ WORKS

Classics Collection Storybook

belongs to

_____

Disney's Sleeping Beauty

CLASSIC STORYBOOK

MOUSE WORKS

Also available in Spanish

© 1986, 1993, 1996 Disney Enterprises, Inc.
Printed in the United States of America
ISBN: 1-57082-731-1
1 3 5 7 9 10 8 6 4 2

Once upon a time, there lived a kind king and gentle queen who longed to have a child. After many years of waiting, they were overjoyed when their daughter was born. They named her Aurora, which means "dawn," because she brightened their lives with happiness just as the sun brightens the day.

A great holiday was proclaimed to celebrate, and visitors were welcomed from far and wide. Among the well-wishers were King Hubert, who ruled the neighboring kingdom, and his young son, Prince Phillip. Both King Hubert and King Stefan, Aurora's father, wished to unite their kingdoms. They declared then and there that the prince and princess would one day marry.

Soon the trumpets sounded, and three sparkling balls of light floated into the room. Out of them emerged Flora, Fauna, and Merryweather, three good fairies who had come to bestow their special gifts upon the infant princess.

Flora approached the cradle first. "Little princess," she said softly, "my gift shall be the gift of beauty...the sun's golden rays in your hair, and lips that are the envy of the red rose."

Now it was Fauna's turn. "My gift shall be the gift of song," she said. And as Fauna waved her wand above the cradle, a flock of colorful birds magically appeared.

But before Merryweather, the third fairy, could present her gift to the baby, a great gust of wind blew open the doors. There was a flash of lightning, a crack of thunder, and then darkness. Suddenly a bright flame burned in the middle of the great hall. It took the shape of a woman.

It was the wicked fairy Maleficent, and she was angry at not being invited to the celebration. To show her displeasure, she placed a curse on the infant princess. "Before the sun sets on her sixteenth birthday," Maleficent promised, "she shall prick her finger on the spindle of a spinning wheel...and die."

The queen cried out in anguish, but Maleficent was unmoved. Her cruel and heartless laugh echoed through the hall.

King Stefan could bear it no longer. "Seize that creature!"
he commanded. But before the guards could reach her,
Maleficent disappeared in a burst of fire and smoke.

Merryweather's powers were not strong enough to undo Maleficent's curse, but she could change it a little. She stepped before the baby and proclaimed, "Not in death, but just in sleep, the fateful prophecy you'll keep, and from this slumber you shall wake, when true love's kiss the spell shall break."

A vision of the sleeping princess appeared before them.

Even with Merryweather's help, King
Stefan still feared for his daughter's life.
To prevent the evil curse from coming true,
he ordered every spinning wheel in the kingdom
to be burned.

But Flora came up with a better plan to protect the princess. "We'll disguise ourselves as peasants," she told the other fairies, "and raise the child deep in the forest. Then, when the curse ends on the princess's sixteenth birthday, we'll return her to the palace."

The king and queen, knowing they had to do everything they could to protect their daughter, agreed. One evening soon after, the fairies slipped away with Aurora.

High on the Forbidden Mountain, Maleficent was losing patience. Year after year, her henchmen scoured the kingdom for the princess without success.

One day Maleficent suddenly realized that for nearly sixteen years her henchmen had been searching for a baby!

"Oh, my pet," the wicked fairy told her raven, "you are my last hope. Circle far and wide. Search for a maiden of sixteen with hair of sunshine gold and lips red as the rose. Go, and do not fail me."

Meanwhile, Princess Aurora
had grown sweet and lovely
under the care of the good
fairies. The three loved the girl,
whom they called Briar Rose,
as if she were their own.

Today Flora, Fauna, and Merryweather were busy making plans for Briar Rose's sixteenth birthday party. They wanted to surprise her, so they sent her out into the forest to pick wild berries while they got everything ready.

Briar Rose wandered through the forest, serenading her animal friends with a lovely melody about the true love she hoped she would one day find.

Nearby, a young prince heard Briar Rose's sweet voice drifting through the trees. He urged his horse Samson to take him to her.

Samson took off in a gallop. When he sailed over a log, though, his master fell off into the water.

"No carrots for you!" scolded the prince. He got up out of the creek and laid his hat, cape, and boots out to dry.

When the prince wasn't looking, Briar Rose's animal friends made off with his hat, cape, and boots.

They dressed up for her,
pretending to be the prince
of her dreams.

Briar Rose continued to sing, pretending to dance with the man she dreamed of loving. She did not hear the prince come up behind her until he joined in her singing.

The prince and Briar Rose fell instantly in love. But when the prince asked her name, Briar Rose remembered the fairies' warning never to speak to strangers. Still, before she left, she invited the prince to come to their cottage that very night.

Meanwhile, back at the cottage, the fairies were having a difficult time with the birthday preparations. The dress Flora was making didn't look quite right.

And Fauna's cake leaned so badly to one side that she had to brace it with a broom. When she did, the icing and the candles slid off the top of the cake and down the broom handle.

The fairies had given up magic, but now they were desperate. They retrieved all the wands from the attic and set to work.

Certain that no one could see them, they set about making everything perfect—with a little help from their magic wands.

Just then, Maleficent's pet raven flew overhead. He saw the colorful sparkles of magic wands shooting out the cottage's chimney. Knowing instantly that the good fairies must live there, he raced to the Forbidden Mountain to tell his mistress that he had found the princess at last.

58

Soon Briar Rose returned home and told the fairies all about the handsome stranger she'd met.

The fairies knew the time had come to tell her the truth. When they were done, they began their long journey back to the palace. It was time to return the princess to the king and queen. As Aurora walked, she could think only of the young man she had met that day.

When the fairies left Aurora alone
for a short time in the palace, a
wisp of light appeared before her.
In a trance, the princess followed it
through a secret panel and up a
winding staircase to a hidden room.

63

Maleficent's voice filled the room. "Touch the spindle! Touch it, I say!" she commanded. The princess obeyed, and pricked her finger on its sharp point.

Meanwhile, the three fairies returned to the room where they had left Aurora for safekeeping. They followed the path to the hidden tower and found Maleficent standing gleefully over the fallen princess.

"The king and queen will be heartbroken when they find out," sobbed Merryweather.

"They're not going to," replied Flora. And then the fairies flew about the palace, putting everyone into a deep sleep.

King Hubert was at the palace that night to celebrate the princess's return. Just before he was about to go to sleep, Flora overheard him trying to tell King Stefan something. It seemed that Prince Phillip was insisting he was going to marry a peasant girl.

With a little more help from the sleepy king, Flora realized that Aurora's young man from the forest was Prince Phillip. As she suspected, he was already arriving at the cottage in the glen.

When the prince entered, he was met by Maleficent and her henchmen. She knew that he alone had the power to undo her curse on Aurora.

Back in her dungeon, Maleficent revealed to the prince that the peasant girl of his dreams was none other than Princess Aurora. The evil fairy taunted Prince Phillip with the news that only he could awaken Aurora, with his kiss. Phillip knew he must somehow escape to save his true love.

At that moment, the good fairies appeared. They released the prince and armed him with the enchanted Shield of Virtue and Sword of Truth. "These weapons will triumph over evil," they told him.

As they fled the dungeon, Prince
Phillip and the fairies encountered
Maleficent's faithful pet raven, who
quickly flew to tell the sorceress of
the prince's escape.

Maleficent's henchmen shot arrows at the
prince, but Flora turned them to flowers.

As Prince Phillip neared the palace, Maleficent put a wall of thorns before him. But he cut the branches with his Sword of Truth.

When the prince neared the castle bridge, Maleficent turned herself into a terrible dragon and blasted him with red-hot flames.

Prince Phillip soon found himself cornered on the edge of a cliff. The fairies rushed to his aid. They sprinkled his sword with fairy dust, saying, "Now Sword of Truth fly swift and sure, that evil die and good endure."

All at once an explosion of fire
knocked the prince's shield away. Phillip
took aim with his sword and hurled it at
the dragon. The beast fell back in agony,
and plunged over the edge of the cliff.

Prince Phillip ran through the palace gates and up to the chamber where Aurora lay. He knelt beside the princess and kissed her gently on the lips. The sleeping beauty awakened and smiled at her prince.

Then everyone else in the kingdom awoke, including King Stefan and his queen. The princess and her parents rushed joyfully into each other's arms, reunited at last.

Soon after, Princess Aurora married Prince Phillip...and they lived happily ever after.